Indi Surfs

Chris Gorman

Brooklyn, NY

Indi
is
a surfer.

She lives
on an island.

The beach is her playground.

The ocean is her swimming pool.

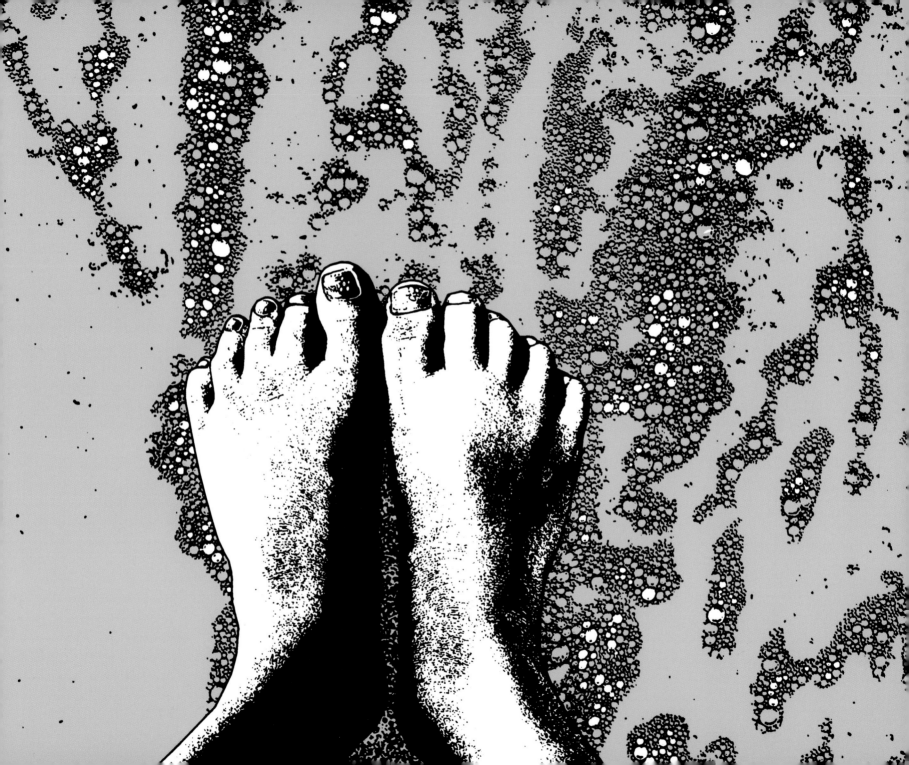

Indi can swim like a fish,

paddle for miles,

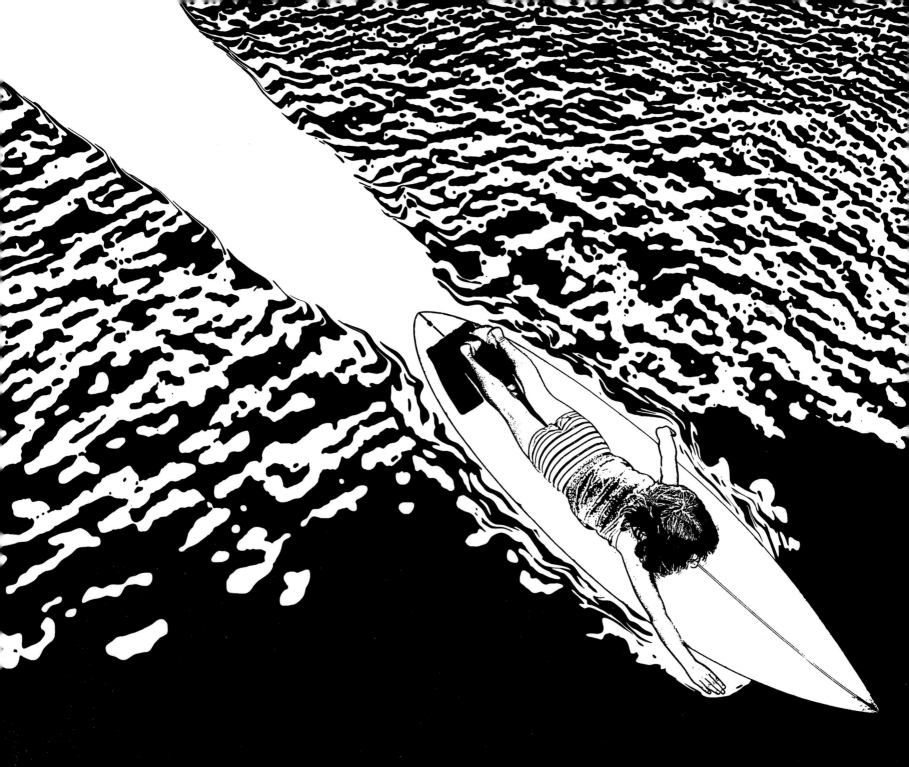

and
dive
under
breaking
waves.

When the ocean is calm, she is patient.

When the surf is big, she is careful.

Big waves, small waves,
Indi loves to ride them all.

Sometimes she falls...

and she falls...

She never gives up.

She paddles back out,

and she tries again.

Watching, waiting, swimming, paddling, and falling. Surfing can be hard.

But when Indi catches her wave...

it's worth it!

This book is for INDI.

Special thanks to Indi, Camille, Toll, Vicki Jacobson, Lisa Blatchley, Tom Gorman, Ryan Hunter, Sean Heneghan, Krzysztof Poluchowicz & Sharyn Rosart.

Wave illustrations inspired by the surf photography of James Parascandola.

© 2015 by Christopher T. Gorman

Published by POW!
a division of powerHouse Packaging & Supply, Inc.
37 Main Street, Brooklyn, NY 11201-1021
info@powkidsbooks.com • www.powkidsbooks.com
www.powerHouseBooks.com • www.powerHousePackaging.com

Library of Congress Control Number: 2014953794

ISBN: 978-1-57687-765-4

10 9 8 7 6 5 4 3 2 1

Printed in Malaysia